Masha and The Bear®

A Spooky Bedtime

Adapted by **Lauren Forte**
Based on the episode **"The Thriller Night"**
written by **Oleg Kuzovkov**

LITTLE, BROWN & COMPANY
LB kids

Little, Brown and Company
Hachette Book Group
1290 Avenue of the Americas, New York, NY 10104
Visit us at lb-kids.com

First Edition: July 2017

LB kids is an imprint of Little, Brown and Company. The LB kids name and logo
are trademarks of Hachette Book Group, Inc.

The publisher is not responsible for websites (or their content)
that are not owned by the publisher.

Library of Congress Control Number 2017932677

ISBNs: 978-0-316-43621-2 (pbk.), 978-0-316-43622-9 (ebook),
978-0-316-43623-6 (ebook), 978-0-316-43624-3 (ebook)

Printed in the United States of America

CW

10 9 8 7 6 5 4 3 2 1

One dark and stormy night, Masha is staying over at the Bear's house. Masha has played all day long. It is time to go to sleep.

"What?" asks Masha. "Go to bed with no bedtime story?"

The Bear helps Masha into his favorite
chair in front of the television. Now she can
watch a fairy tale to help her fall asleep.

When the Bear goes upstairs to make her bed, Masha changes the channel. The show he put on is boring. She chooses something that is not boring at all—it's scary!

The show is too scary! Masha hides her face and doesn't see the Bear come back into the living room. When she looks up at him, she thinks she sees a monster!

Masha screams! The Bear screams! They both scared each other. "Oh, it's you," Masha says once she calms down.

She feels a little silly.

When the Bear sees what she is watching, he
turns off the TV. He tells her not to watch scary
movies. They can be frightening!

The Bear tucks Masha in to her little cot. Then, he hops into his own bed. Outside, the wind and rain continue. Lightning flashes and thunder crashes!

Masha can't sleep. First, she hears a creaky noise. "Bear, what is that?" she asks. But the Bear tells her not to worry.

Then she hears the rain and asks, "Bear, what's over there?" Again, he tells her not to worry.

But when she hears a clanging sound on the roof, she cries, "Bear?!"

The Bear realizes how
worried Masha is. The
movie must have scared
her more than he thought.
He feels bad, so he goes
to check out the sound.

The Bear climbs out onto the roof and realizes the clanging sound is only a rusty TV antenna swinging in the wind.

Suddenly, lightning strikes! The Bear gets
a shock and falls to the ground. *Ouch!*

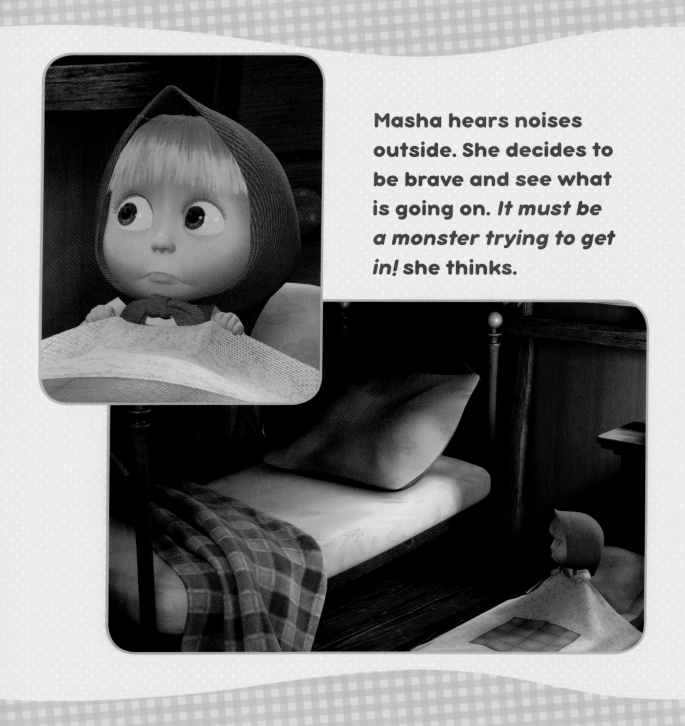

Masha hears noises outside. She decides to be brave and see what is going on. *It must be a monster trying to get in!* she thinks.

Masha sets a trap. She lifts the cellar door. As soon as the "monster" bursts in, he falls into the basement. She got him!

Then she hears a noise by the fireplace!
Is the monster trying to get in that way now?

The Bear tries to climb down the chimney. Masha is scared by the noises.

The Bear forgot that there's a fire in the fireplace.
Once he gets too close, he shouts, *"Oooh eeeh aaah!"*
He climbs back out of the chimney—and fast!

The Bear runs around the yard, cooling his burned bottom in the rain puddles. He is not happy. And he's had enough!

The Bear climbs in the bedroom window. But he slips on a ball, falls down the stairs, and ends up in the fridge! Slowly, he pushes open the door...

...only to be hit on the head with bananas!
"Go away, scary monster!" Masha hollers.

"*Shhhhhh!*" says the Bear.

"Oh, it's only you," Masha says once she calms down. She feels silly all over again.

Together, the Bear and Masha settle down in his favorite chair. All safe, they slowly fall asleep. Sometimes a good snuggle is better than a bedtime story.